DOG DIARIES

SWEETIE

DOG DIARIES

#1: GINGER
A puppy-mill survivor in search of a *furever* family

#2: BUDDY
The first Seeing Eye guide dog

#3: BARRY
Legendary rescue dog of the Great Saint Bernard Hospice

#4: TOGO
Unsung hero of the 1925 Nome Serum Run

#5: DASH
One of two dogs to travel to the New World
aboard the *Mayflower*

#6: SWEETIE
George Washington's "perfect" foxhound

DOG DIARIES

SWEETIE

by KATE KLIMO • ILLUSTRATED BY TIM JESSELL

RANDOM HOUSE 🏠 NEW YORK

The author and editor would like to thank Mary V. Thompson, MA, Litt D, research historian, the Fred W. Smith National Library for the Study of George Washington; and Dr. Robert D. Smith and Polly Dorsey Smith, founders of the American Foxhound Club and all-breed judges for the American Kennel Club, for their assistance in the preparation of this book.

This is a work of fiction. All incidents and dialogue, and all characters with the exception of some well-known historical and public figures, are products of the author's imagination and are not to be construed as real. Where real-life historical or public figures appear, the situations, incidents, and dialogues concerning those persons are fictional and are not intended to depict actual events or to change the fictional nature of the work. In all other respects, any resemblance to persons living or dead is entirely coincidental.

Text copyright © 2015 by Kate Klimo
Cover art and interior illustrations copyright © 2015 by Tim Jessell
Photographs courtesy of Private Collection/Peter Newark American pictures/Bridgeman Images, p. ix; Mount Vernon Ladies' Association, p. 150

Visit us on the Web! randomhousekids.com

Educators and librarians, for a variety of teaching tools, visit us at
RHTeachersLibrarians.com

Library of Congress Cataloging-in-Publication Data
Klimo, Kate.
Sweetie / by Kate Klimo ; illustrated by Tim Jessell.—First edition.
pages cm.—(Dog diaries ; #6)
Summary: "George Washington's foxhound Sweetlips narrates the story of her master's transformation from farmer to Father of our Country."—Provided by publisher.
Includes bibliographical references.
ISBN 978-0-385-39240-2 (trade)—ISBN 978-0-385-39241-9 (lib. bdg.)—
ISBN 978-0-385-39242-6 (ebook)
1. American foxhound—Juvenile fiction. [1. American foxhound—Fiction.
2. Dogs—Fiction. 3. Washington, George, 1732–1799—Fiction. 4. United States—History—Revolution, 1775–1783—Fiction.] I. Jessell, Tim, illustrator. II. Title.
PZ10.3.K686Sw 2015 [Fic]—dc23 2014006104

Printed in the United States of America

10 9 8 7 6 5

First Edition

For Faith Moeckel,
who lighted the way to Sweetlips
—K.K.

For our dogs, who add so much to our lives
—T.J.

CONTENTS

The First Gentlemen of Virginia by John Ward Dunsmore, 1909

THE PERFECT FOXHOUND

August 6, 1768, dawned hot and muggy, just another summer's day on the Mansion House Farm. Over at the gristmill, millers were grinding wheat. Carpenters mended a hole in the roof of the toolshed. In the kitchen yard, two servant women stirred a pot of lard, lye, and beeswax to make soap. And in the kennel down by the river, the she-hound known as Lady brought forth into this world four pups: Vulcan, Rover, Searcher, and me—Sweetlips.

Other than the red spots on my white coat, I had no special markings that might have told the world: "Behold! One day, this dog will play a role on the stage of history." To the ignorant eye, I was just another pup in the kennel. But I knew I was different. Did my brothers see this? Alas, no. I must say that those first weeks were a day-to-day struggle. My siblings seemed to feel that Mother's milk was wasted on the likes of me. Blind and clumsy though I was, I managed to suckle while fending off my littermates with a flurry of well-aimed kicks.

Good for you, Sweetie! my mother cheered. *A lady must fend for herself.*

Even then, tussling was not to my taste. I disliked having my fur rucked up or my coat soiled. But I would not let those rude boys get in the way of that sweet, warm stream of milk as it gushed past my lips into my mouth. You might wonder, is this how I came by the name of Sweetlips? For the answer to that question, you would have to ask the Colonel, my master. He named every hound—Forester, Sancho, Ringwood, Lawlor, Tipsy, Sentwell, Chanter, Singer, Busy, Music, Pixey, Maiden, and on and on—according to his whim. Everything of note that happened in the kennel, that man set down in his papers. The Colonel was a most careful and exacting man.

I remember clearly the morning the Colonel came to the kennel with his new hunt master, Will Lee. We hounds all lined up along the fence. When the men swung open the gate, there was a great deal of hurling and burling to get close to the Colonel. I stayed at my mother's side and watched. My eyes might have been newly open, but they took it all in. And what I saw, I liked.

The Colonel had a way about him that made a dog pay attention. Perhaps it was the straightness of him, like a sturdy tree, long of trunk and limb. Perhaps it was the calm air he gave off, as if nothing bad could ever happen around him. He was clad in leather boots and breeches and a white shirt. Will Lee was similarly garbed, but he was smaller, stouter, and dark of skin. The Colonel bent down. His long fingers sifted through our fur.

Pray tell, Mother, what is he doing? I asked.

Searching for signs of the mange, she said.

Before I could ask her what the mange was, the Colonel stopped and stared hard at Sancho. He was bent nearly in half, gnawing at his lower back. When Sancho felt the Colonel's eyes on him, he unbent. His ears drooped.

Begging your pardon, Colonel. I was just tending to some fleas.

There was an angry red patch on his back. The Colonel pointed it out to Will.

"That is the mange if ever I saw it," said the Colonel. The two men murmured to one another. Then they moved on to Countess. The Colonel lifted her tail and peered beneath it. "We will have to keep an eye out and shut her up when she comes proud," he said to Will.

What is proud? I asked my mother. (How little I knew then!)

Her time for mating, Mother replied.

Just the other day, I had seen the Colonel take away another she-hound. He had declared her proud, too. At the time, I thought that she was being punished for putting on airs. He locked her away in the barn, then brought her back a few days later.

Why did he lock her away? I asked my mother.

The Colonel breeds us according to his own plan, Mother explained. *He wants to make sure we ladies mate with the gents he chooses to get the right sort of puppy. He mated me with Forester to get the likes of you. But sometimes, it is his plan that a female have no puppies at all. Especially if he doesn't think she will have the right sort. After all, it's not as if this kennel isn't crowded enough as it is.*

How right my mother was! Day or night, there was never a moment when I was alone. The kennel teemed with hounds of all shapes and sizes. They fought over sticks and favors. They tussled and rassled in a most unseemly fashion. They snoozed and dreamt. They growled and howled and scratched and shook and snorted and muttered and did their business where they liked. The kennel was halfway up a grassy hillside. Below us flowed the wide Potomac River. Above us loomed

6

the Colonel's home, the Mansion House. Off to one side I could just make out the barns and the paddocks. How these far-off places fascinated me!

The barns and paddocks are where the Colonel keeps the horses and other animals, my mother explained. *We hounds may be the Colonel's first love, but he does have a deep fondness for horses.*

I had seen enough hounds to last me a lifetime. But I had yet to lay eyes on a horse. At a mere month old, the kennel was my world. Mother said that the kennel had everything I would ever need. There was food aplenty. Inside a rude shack, we sheltered from storms. There was even a stream running through the fenced yard. Just the other day, I had dipped my nose into it by accident and—lo!—discovered it was very nearly as tasty as Mother's milk. Still, I wanted more than food and shelter and drink. I wanted adventure!

Feeling a thirst coming on, I worked my way over to the stream. I was just lowering my head to drink, when I felt a rude tug on the scruff of my neck. Suddenly—what was this?—I was rising high into the air. My heart skittered like a beetle bug in my chest as I found myself face to face with the Colonel! His pale eyes examined me. A smile played on his thin lips.

I gave out with an indignant growl. *I beg your*

pardon! Sir, why do you trifle with me?

"This would be the female from the most recent litter. I call her Sweetlips," the Colonel said as he dangled me in the air before Will Lee. "She just might be my finest hound yet."

"She looks very good, sir," Will said.

"Nay, Billy. She looks *perfect*," the Colonel said.

As quickly as he had picked me up, he set me back down. I shook out my coat so hard that I fell flat on my face.

Mother nudged me to my feet, smoothing the rumpled fur on my neck.

The Colonel is right, as always, she said. *You are perfect.*

But what does it mean to be perfect? I asked.

To the Colonel's way of thinking, perfect means bred for the chase, my mother said.

I cocked my head. *The chase?* The very sound

of the word made me want to lift my nose to the sky and howl.

Chasing after foxes, my mother said. *That is what we foxhounds are bred to do.*

Might I chase after a fox today? I asked. Whatever in the world a fox was, I was ready to chase one to the ends of the earth.

She laughed softly and washed me with her big warm tongue. *Your time will come, Sweetie.*

The next morning, the Colonel and Will arrived early. Curiously, the dogs did not line up at the fence for their usual rowdy welcome. Instead, they hung back, tails and ears drooping, their eyes filled with woe.

The Colonel and Will wore dark aprons over their clothing. Their hands were hidden in thick gloves. Each man set down a steaming bucket. My nose told me that it was not delicious food in those buckets. It was something bad that smelled even worse. The fur along my spine stood up.

"Now then, my fine hounds!" the Colonel called out. "It is time for the anointing!"

Instantly, a boisterous baying rose. Do you know what baying is? It is like howling, only more musical. And the music this day was tragic.

What's happening? I asked my mother.

My three brothers crowded around, echoing my question.

From the smell of it, we are about to be dipped, our mother said.

Dipped? I asked. *In that stuff? Perish the thought!*

Sancho is to blame, said our father, Forester, with a deep growl. *The rest of us are in fine fettle.*

Nevertheless, every hound and puppy in this kennel is about be bathed, said my mother with a sad shake of her head.

Now see here, whined Sancho. *It's not as if I tried to get the mange. I caught it from one of those Fairfax hounds, I tell you.*

Indignant, I asked, *What if we don't want to be dipped?*

Ha! The Colonel's word is law, said Vulcan as he butted me with his head.

It is for our own good, said Rover and Searcher, each grabbing one of my ears in their mouths and tugging.

My mother added, *It's the Colonel's own special recipe. Hog's fat and brimstone.*

Ugh! I shook my brothers off. The very words— hog's fat and brimstone—made my fur curl. *What is that?*

Hogs are great fat animals that eat constantly and live in their own filth, Forester explained. *Brimstone is something very powerful. The most powerful thing about it is its stench. You would not believe it.*

It is meant to cure us of the mange and keep us from getting it, Mother said.

If it doesn't kill us first, Forester muttered.

Pilot was the first to go. He was the leader among us hounds. If he willingly went, the rest of us would follow. The wily Pilot, however, knew better. He tried to bolt. But Will was too fast. He lunged after Pilot and dragged him over to the bucket. With sponge and brush, the two men covered Pilot from head to tail in the dreadful dip. I scarcely recognized Pilot when they were through. There he stood: a miserable, slimy, shivering heap of fur. As soon as they let him loose, he shook himself out, spraying men and dogs alike.

"Who's next, Colonel?" Will said, wiping his brow.

"Fetch me Forester," said the Colonel.

I did not wait to see my poor father being hauled to the bucket. I took myself off and hid in the farthest corner of the shed. From my hiding place, I could hear one hound after another being dragged to the bucket and dipped. The air reeked of brimstone and misery. Then came the puppies. They whimpered as they went. When they were dipped, they yelped and squealed as if their tails had been caught in the gate hinge. How I longed for it all to be over!

"That should do it, sir," Will said.

The Colonel was silent for a moment. Then he said, "I think not, Billy. Where is Sweetlips?"

A Foxhound at the Tea Party

Hearing my name, I went as still as a stone.

"Sweetlips!" the Colonel called out. But Sweetlips would not stir. No, indeed. Not if it meant being dipped.

I felt a tingling on the back of my neck, followed by the weight of a big warm hand. The Colonel had crawled all the way into the back of the shack to reach me. "Here's my naughty little Sweetie," he said. Easing himself out, he dropped me into the bucket. I thrashed about, too stunned to utter a sound. Then he lifted me high, dripping, and held me before his face.

I cast him a reproachful look. *How could you? I thought I was perfect as I was!*

His thin lips widened into a grin. His pale eyes sparkled with mischief.

"Her first anointment! And she let out nary a yelp! I tell you, Billy, this little hound is fast becoming my favorite."

For days, we hounds staggered about the kennel in a dull fog. The Colonel's treatment might have banished mange, but it had also temporarily destroyed our ability to smell. A dog without a nose might as well be deaf and blind. Gradually, our noses returned to duty as our nostrils filled with a sweet and tangy scent.

That is the smell of apples ripening, Mother said.

It means that the best hunting time of the year is nigh.

Life returned to normal. My brothers took to racing one another from one end of the kennel yard to the other. I sat and cleaned myself with my tongue, running my teeth and tongue over each toe until my claws glowed and the fur of my feet shone a dazzling white.

What do you think you are? A cat or a hound? Rover asked me.

I am a lady, if you must know, I said to my brother. *And a lady looks after herself.*

One bright, crisp day, a young woman came among us. She waded through the hounds over to my mother. "Which of your pups is Sweetlips, Lady? The Colonel has told me I may bring her out to play," she said.

Mother looked up at her and smiled, her tail

thumping the dirt. *This is Patsy,* she said to me. *She is a gentle sort: the daughter of the Colonel's mate, the Missus. Patsy is the light of their life. Go with her, Sweetie,* she said as she nudged me with her nose. *It is time you laid eyes on the world outside the kennel.*

"Sweetlips!" Cooing softly, Patsy lifted me up in gentle hands. "Aren't you the sweetest little one? Such a fitting name! My step-papa named you well."

Overcome by sudden affection, I licked her cheek. My, but she tasted sour!

Patsy seemed to know this. "Forgive me, Sweet-lips. I have been ailing of late," she said to me as she unlatched the gate.

Usually, the hounds surged for the opening and tried to escape. But today, Pilot held them back.

She is frail. Let her pass, he growled.

A dark-skinned young woman awaited her out-side, armed with a stick. At first, I feared she meant me harm. Then I understood. Like Pilot, she wanted to protect Patsy.

"This is Rose," Patsy said. "She is my faithful body servant and shadow. She must go everywhere with me these days because I have the falling sick-ness. No one knows when I will keel over and have a fit! They are quite dreadful, these fits. My eyes roll back in my head, my mouth foams, and my limbs flail in a most unladylike display."

I heaved a sympathetic sigh. Then I licked

her face again, hoping to clean away the sickness as Sancho had tried to lick away the mange. She laughed. "That tickles," she said. And yet she did not push me away.

Rose trailing behind, Patsy carried me up the hill, away from the kennel. I looked back over her shoulder. The hounds pressed themselves to the fence slats and peered out at me.

I heard my mother's voice say, *You do me proud, Sweetie!*

Pilot bayed, *Where do you think you're going, young upstart?*

I knew exactly where I was going: out into the world! So great were the hustle and bustle all around me that I did not know where to look first.

"Everyone here works," Patsy said as she walked up the hill. "Except perhaps myself and my brother, Jacky. We, alas, are idle. I, because of illness. He, because he is a lazy dear. Papa encourages him to attend to his studies, but I fear he would rather hunt and fish and play cards."

Men and women, many dark-skinned like Rose and Will Lee, moved about. Some hauled loads on their backs. Others carried baskets and buckets and crates.

"These are our slaves," Patsy explained to me. "They have come—I fear against their will—from far away. Papa feeds and clothes and houses them and expects them to work hard in return."

Down by the river, more slaves were building a wooden wharf. In the distance, I saw the Colonel. He was astride a long-legged, long-nosed beast.

"Doesn't Papa look splendid on horseback?" Patsy said.

So this was a horse! The Colonel did, indeed, cut a fine figure, sitting astride the horse. Together, horse and man were like a single noble creature. The Colonel lifted a hand and waved to us. Then the horse spun around and bore him off into the trees. I squirmed. I wanted to go with them. I belonged alongside those two.

But Patsy held me all the more tightly. "Not yet, little one," she sighed. "One day, you will go with the Colonel on his rounds. He makes them every day. He is a very busy man with many holdings. Between the houses and the land, he has at least one hundred slaves to oversee: millers, blacksmiths, tanners, carpenters, field hands. Then there are the fields of wheat and corn and vegetables and orchards. And let's not forget the animals— sheep, hogs, cows, chickens, ducks. Not to mention keeping all the clocks wound. It is a wonder he ever has time to hunt or attend balls or barbecues or do any of the things he so delights in doing.

My mother says that Papa is as busy as the mayor of a city! I think he must be busier, for surely no mayor ever had so many mouths to feed nor bodies to clothe."

She was breathless by the time we got to the Mansion House. The building rose up before me, impossibly grand. And yet, I knew I belonged here more than in the kennel. On the lawn lay a blanket spread with cups and plates. On it sat a circle of small people. Their bodies were stiff and their eyes dead and still.

"These are my doll babies," Patsy said to me. "This one here is Annabelle. She comes all the way from England. Papa ordered her special for me. He is a lover of fine things, and most fine things come from England. Isn't her gown beautiful? Today, we're having a tea party. And you, my dear little one, are the guest of honor."

Although I would later attend many a tea party with the Colonel, this was my first. I was so grateful to be invited that I licked Patsy's face again. She giggled. "You are most welcome, Sweetlips. But, first, I must fetch dear Mama," she said. "She will be in the kitchen yard, no doubt. Sometimes I think she works harder than the Colonel. Overseeing everything that has to do with the Mansion House is my mama's job. Mending, cooking, making soap, stocking the provisions, polishing the silver, airing the bedding. It makes me dizzy just thinking of it. So many visitors come here and she welcomes them all."

Patsy carried me behind a high wooden fence next to the house. In the kitchen yard, dark-skinned women bustled in and out of a group of smaller buildings, some not larger than our kennel shack.

In one building, a woman worked her fingers

in a wad of gooey white stuff, while another sliced apples. Something smelled warm and delicious. So this was the source of the mouthwatering aromas that wafted downhill to the kennel!

"She's not in the kitchen," said Patsy.

In the next building, I smelled something meaty. *May we please go in there?* I asked, trying not to whimper.

Patsy inhaled deeply. "That is the smokehouse," she said. "My mama's smoked hams are famous throughout Virginia."

Then came a building that smelled hot and steamy and clean.

"The laundry room," Patsy said. "Here she is!"

A short, comfortable-looking woman emerged from the steam. She fanned herself with her apron. I could tell, just by the smell of her, that she was the Colonel's mate, the Missus.

"Try as we might, we cannot seem to get the port stains out of my good linen tablecloth," the Missus said.

"It's time for my tea party, Mama," said Patsy. "My new little friend, Sweetie, and I have come to fetch you."

The Missus chucked me beneath the chin with a warm reddened finger. "Isn't she the cunning one?"

Patsy whispered in my ear, "My mama's heart belongs to a little spaniel dog named Pompey, but she will not mind if you come to our tea party."

We returned with the Missus to the blanket. Patsy set me down next to one of the doll babies. The Missus and Patsy sat on either side of me, their skirts spread prettily on the grass.

"Shall I pour?" Patsy said.

"Please do, my dear," said the Missus.

Patsy tipped a shiny pot into a cup and handed it to her mother. Then she tipped the pot into another cup and placed it in front of me.

"Oh, I forgot. You take your tea sweet, don't you, Sweetie? Naturally! You must have sugar . . . and plenty of cream." She fiddled some more with the cup, then set it back down before me.

But when I dipped my nose into the cup, I found it empty!

What folly was this?

Patsy stroked me as she said to her mother, "I do hope I may come with you and Papa to Belvoir on Sunday. I am so fearfully bored here, I am reduced to childish games such as this."

"We will have to see what Dr. Rumney says," said the Missus. "Remember what happened the last time?"

Patsy dropped her chin to her chest. "I had a fit

in the coach on the way home," she said in a soft voice.

"There, there. All will be well, I'm sure." The Missus patted Patsy tenderly on the shoulder. "Let us speak of more cheerful matters!"

While the ladies rattled on, I looked around the circle of doll babies. My gaze fell on the fine Annabelle. Surely, I deserved fine things as much as Patsy did. Annabelle stared at me with her dull eyes. Her head, I could see, was as hard as stone. But she had a soft, fragrant body. I stood up and fastened my mouth around her neck, then off I trotted across the lawn with my head held high! I found a spot behind a bush and knelt to gloat over my new prize.

Patsy cried out, "Sweetie has made off with my doll baby!"

Soon, Rose came stalking me. "Give me the

doll baby, Sweetie," she said in a low, coaxing voice.

I stared up at her warily. Then I grasped the doll in my mouth and trotted on down the hill. I would show off my new prize for all my kennel mates to admire. But Rose had other ideas. She pounced and caught me up in her arms.

"Gotcha, you furry little thief!" she said.

With a rough tug, she tore the doll from my jaws. There came a loud ripping sound. Poor doll! Her beautiful dress hung in tatters! And it was all my fault! Had I left her at the tea party, this would never have happened.

"You're in a sight of trouble now, little hound dog," Rose muttered to me as she marched me back to Patsy. I bowed my head. I would be returning to the kennel under a cloud of shame. Mother would be so disappointed in me.

But what should we see but Patsy and the Missus sitting on the lawn, doubled over and laughing. Tears streamed from their eyes.

Patsy caught her breath and sat up. She took the doll and smoothed her tattered skirts. "Thank you, Rose. There's no real harm done. I daresay that's what comes of inviting a foxhound to a tea party."

THE LINE OF THE FOX

I was a year old when the strange dog came one night. Straightaway, I knew there was something not quite right about him. Sometimes hounds would escape from the kennel and try to survive on their own in the woods. But after having to scratch up their own food, day after day, they usually came back, dragging their tails. After a thorough delousing, the Colonel always took them back. He was that kind of man. Strict, but forgiving. Was this, then, I wondered, one of those wayward dogs?

Lawlor poked his nose through the gap between the gate and fence and growled at the stranger, *Stay away from us.* Pilot might have been our leader. But Lawlor fancied himself the watchdog-in-chief.

The strange dog crept closer, fangs bared.

Maybe you didn't hear me the first time! Lawlor struggled to work his way through the gap.

Stay inside the fence! Pilot barked. *I like not the looks of that dog.*

Nor did I. His eyes were glassy. His mouth was white and foaming. And he walked with a peculiar stiff-legged gait. I backed off. But Lawlor wanted to challenge him. After a great deal of wiggling, he managed to squeeze through the gap between the gate and fence. My brother Rover, never very bright, slipped through the gap after Lawlor. He and Lawlor circled warily around the intruder.

With a vicious snarl, the stranger sprang at Lawlor. Rover launched himself into the melee, and soon all that the rest of us could see was a blur of fur and fangs. Altogether, we must have set up quite a hullabaloo. Soon, light filled the windows of the Mansion House. It was not long before the Colonel came stalking down, clad in his nightshirt, holding a rifle.

He slapped his leg. "Lawlor! Rover! BACK OFF! COME!" he shouted over their snarling. He kicked Lawlor, and the hound skulked away, followed by Rover. Then the Colonel chased the strange dog out of our sight. A few moments later, we heard the loud report of the Colonel's rifle, followed by a yelp. Then silence.

We saw no more of the stranger. But he had left his mark. Both Lawlor and Rover had been bitten. Suspecting the dog had been suffering from the dread disease known as rabies, the Colonel treated the two unfortunate hounds to another of his own home remedies. It was liverwort and black pepper mixed with the blood of a bittern bird. From the way they choked and gagged down their daily doses, it must have been most unpleasant. That—combined with the cold bath they were treated to before every meal for a month—made those two dogs rue the day they ever tangled with that character. But the rabies madness never came upon them. For this, as for so many things, we had the Colonel to thank.

Not long after that incident, Dr. Cleveland came and took the dogs Music, Patsy, Jacky, and Maiden away. I never liked Dr. Cleveland. He puffed on a foul, wet cigar, and his hands smelled of suffering animals. But I liked him even less when Music, Patsy, Jacky, and Maiden came back to the kennel a-hurting. They curled up in the dirt and immediately started licking themselves. When I came close, I saw that their stomachs were stitched up like the seam on a pair of leather breeches!

You are wounded! I gasped.

Music lifted her head from the stitching. *It is not as bad as it looks,* she said. *It itches more than it hurts. The doctor has fixed us so we won't have any more pups.*

Not so long ago, Countess had whelped nine puppies. One of the slaves had come in the night and taken them away. I do not know what happened to those pups. But I do know they were too young to have been taken away from their mother. We never saw them again.

I had yet to go proud myself, but Mother said I would any day now. When that happened, would the doctor take me away and stitch me up? Or would I be allowed to whelp, only to have some-one come in the night and take my puppies away?

Pilot must have sensed my unease. *Don't worry, Sweetlips,* he said. *The Colonel's going to want any litter of yours.*

The Colonel wanted me to hunt, too, or so he said. But each time Will came to take out the hounds to hunt, he snubbed me. Just when I had almost given up hope, Will came for me one morning.

"Let's see how you take to training, Sweetie," he said.

Had my time come, at long last?

Out on the lawn, he raised his hand and said, "Sit."

At first, I did not know what he meant. I wagged my tail. I barked. I spun in circles. I pranced ever so prettily on my hind legs. But he wanted none of that. When, out of sheer exhaustion, I finally sank to my haunches, he said, "That's my girl!" in a loud and happy voice. He then tossed me a bit of meat. Soon, I knew to plant my hindquarters and wait for the meat when he said *sit*. I didn't always get the meat. But I got it often enough that I always sat, just in case.

Then he walked some distance away from me and said, "Come."

I sat and stared at him. "Come," he repeated, again and again. I went on sitting. Finally, he came and grabbed my collar. He pulled me over to the spot where he had been standing when he had said the word. That's how, in time, I came to understand the meaning of the command *come*.

Sometimes he did not want me to come. He wished me to stay where I was. This confused me at first. But after a while, I cottoned on. In later years, the Colonel did not even have to say the words. All he had to do was look at me and smile, and I would come; look at me with a small frown, and I would stay. That's how it would come to be between the Colonel and me. We would have an understanding.

Another day, Will brought to me an item to sniff.

My, but it smelled gamey!

"This is the pelt of a fox," he said.

A fox! At last! Pointy nose, bushy tail, fascinating scent.

He attached a string to the fox pelt and dragged it behind him as he trotted across the lawn. I chased after him. When I lunged to bite the pelt, Will said, "Sit. Stay." He dragged it away. It took all my self-control not to fall upon it. I sat and stayed. But I lifted my head and bayed. Will laughed.

Again, Will made me stay. And, again, he went off dragging the pelt—this time in the direction of the woods. When he came back, the pelt was gone. I stared at him, tail wagging, eyes hopeful. *Where is the fox pelt? What have you done with it?*

Will held his hands beneath my nose. "Find the fox, Sweetie!" he said in a high, eager voice.

I filled my nose with the gamey scent. And— just like that!—I was off and running, at long last doing what I had been put on this earth to do: to follow the line of the fox! That fox pelt led me on a wild chase along the riverbank and up into the woods. I had never been in the woods before. I was surrounded by distractions: trees and birds and squirrels and rabbits. But I would not be put off my mission. I followed that trail until it dead-ended at the base of a great tree. I looked up. The fox pelt dangled from a branch. I jumped up on

the tree trunk, trying in vain to reach *it*. I lifted my head and bayed the age-old song of all hunting hounds:

I have found the fox!

The pelt lesson was followed by many a brisk walk with Will through the woods. We followed the well-beaten paths the Colonel favored in the hunt. They wound all over the Mansion House Farm property and onto the surrounding lands. These paths led us through deep woods and brambles, across streams and rivulets, over stone walls and hedges, and through muddy sloughs. Sometimes Will brought along a rifle. Without a word of warning, he would fire it close to my head. At first, this made me run around in circles, yelping at the painful ringing in my ears. But soon, I grew hardened to the sound and remained calm and composed. When I returned to the kennel, I busied myself cleaning my feet and coat. The woods were wonderful. But they were also filthy.

My first hunt took place on a morning when the grass was brittle with frost and my breath came out in puffy clouds. Will came and got Pilot and Tipsy—and me! He had finally chosen me! From head to tail, I trembled with excitement. He attached leads to us, and we bounded alongside Will. We came upon the Colonel sitting astride his big dark horse. With him were two other mounted men, who I would come to know as Mr. Fairfax and Mr. Alexander. Riding a pony was the boy called Jacky, son of the Missus and brother of Patsy. I must confess that I had never taken to Jacky. He had snake eyes. But for the Colonel's sake, I was always civil to him.

"Sit," Will told us, after releasing us from our leads. We three sat while Will climbed upon his own mount. "This is my horse, Chinkling. Don't worry, Sweetie. He won't harm you. You'll be working together."

But I wasn't fretting about Chinkling. It was the Colonel's horse that worried me. Up close, he was enormous. His hooves were bigger than my head! He snorted and swung his head away from me in disgust. *Upstart!* he grumbled.

Don't mind Blueskin, said Pilot. *He is the Colonel's favorite hunting mount. He fancies himself above the rest of us. Just stay out from under his hooves and you'll fare well.*

"Shall we go a-hunting, then, fellows?" shouted the Colonel. His cheeks were rosy, and his eyes shone. His horse pranced in place. The breath of horse, hound, and man fogged the frosty air.

Will put a golden horn to his lips and blew. Hounds bayed, horses whinnied, men sent up a cheer. Will heeled his horse, and we hounds took to the path. *Follow me,* said Pilot. *And do what I do.*

Noses to the ground, heads sweeping back and forth casting about for a scent, we three hounds moved forward along one of the many paths I had walked with Will. But how much faster was our pace now! My heart thudded. Pilot was leading. I kept his tail in view. Soon, I became so caught up seeking a scent that I was in a world of my own. Yet in that world, I caught not a whisper of the scent of fox.

Over here! said Pilot as he veered off the path. Tipsy and I followed him into the deep woods.

"Are you onto a fox, Pilot?" Will asked eagerly as he stayed with us. Behind him, I heard the other horses crashing through the thicket. We scrambled over rotten logs and through bushes and high grass. My ears grew heavy with burs and brambles. I am sure I looked a sight, but still I followed Pilot. I did not smell a fox, but surely he must have. We had run for quite some time, when, suddenly, a great stag with antlers as broad and heavy as tree limbs leapt out of the brush before us and fled into the undergrowth.

After it! Tipsy cried. *A deer is as good as a fox, I always say.*

Not to the Colonel, it isn't, said Pilot glumly. *Hold up, you two.*

Will arrived, panting from the run, the flanks of his horse lathered. He wagged his head in disappointment. "This sorry hound started a deer!" he shouted back to the Colonel.

From behind us, the Colonel burst into a good-natured laugh. "No matter! He led us on a merry chase!"

Will looked down at us in disgust. "Where to now, dogs?" he asked. "And this time, it had better be after a fox."

Pilot sat, ears drooping. I could tell he felt badly about the deer. I was just lifting my hind leg to brush away a tick, when I caught it. I sat up and sniffed at the gamey hint in the air that whispered, *fox, fox, fox.* I turned tail and headed off toward it.

Where do you think you're going? Pilot called.

I did not answer. Nor did I stop. Faint as it was, the scent was as clear to me as if Will were pulling the fox pelt just ahead of me. And, just as with the fox pelt, there was a line attaching my nose to the fox. It dragged me along behind it. I was powerless to do anything but go with it.

Soon, Pilot, Tipsy, Will, and the hunters were hard at my heels. The stronger the scent, the faster I

ran: scrambling over walls, squeezing under fences and hedges, slogging through mud, dashing across fields. Behind me, I heard the thunder of hooves, the snort of horses, the creak of saddle leather. Obstacles that the other two hounds and I crawled under the horses leapt over. And the higher the obstacle, the louder the Colonel crowed his delight.

"After him, Sweetie!" the Colonel cried.

I sensed the fox somewhere ahead of us. He knew we were on his tail. He zigzagged to throw us

off his scent. He circled behind us more than once. By the time I had doubled back to follow him, he was in the lead again. That fox was a tease, daring me to catch him! A sharp stick gouged me, but did I care? I cared only about catching up to that fox. I was running so fast, Pilot and Tipsy howled after me to slow down or wait up. But I shook off their pleas. I had ears only for the wind, the branches as they snapped in my path, the underbrush as it crackled beneath my feet, my heart as it raced.

I was wet to the skin and bleeding from my side when I treed the fox in an area I would come to know as Dogue Run. He stared down at me with big sly eyes as he hugged the bark halfway up an oak.

Ha! I have you now, I said, crouching at the foot of the tree.

I lifted my head. I saw that the sun was high in

the sky. I had been chasing this fox the better part of a morning. I bayed to alert the others.

I have found the fox!

The horses wheeled about, in a muddy lather. The riders were red-faced, breathless, and very merry. Pilot and Tipsy, on the other paw, looked as if they had been dragged tail first through a swamp.

Good work, said Pilot, panting.

For a beginner, added Tipsy, flipping a muddy ear out of his eyes.

"Ha!" said the Colonel. He leapt down from his mount and ruffled the damp fur on my head. "Methinks the lady is a born foxhunter. Capital work, Sweetie!" Then he saw my bleeding side. "Billy, see to that scratch." He slapped the tree trunk with his riding crop. The fox scrambled down the trunk and scampered away.

"Stay," Will ordered us in a low voice.

Did you see that? I growled to Pilot. *He set the fox free. After all my hard work!*

Tipsy sighed and scratched himself. *He does that sometimes. Especially when the fox is male. As a rule, vixens he'll shoot. Males, he often spares.*

It isn't the kill he enjoys so much as the chase, said Pilot. *Charging around his land on one of his trusty steeds.*

From that day on, I went hunting with the Colonel once a week, sometimes more. We rode in all weather and at all times of day. Sometimes on the hunt, I never scented a single fox. Other times, a fox would lead us on for miles only to go to ground. Then there were the times when I would tree the fox and the Colonel would kill it. Afterward, the men rode back to the Mansion House— or over to Belvoir, if Mr. Fairfax was riding that day—and feast. Either Will or the Colonel always gave me a marrowbone as a reward for my efforts.

A few days after that first hunt, I became proud for the first time. Will took me and locked me up in an empty stall in the barn. "Colonel wants to save you for hunting," he said. "Not for whelping."

That was how it came to pass that I never gave birth to a single litter of puppies. Besides the love of the hunt, that was another thing I had in common with the Colonel. Neither of us ever had a single pup of our own. But what, I ask you, did I need of litters, when I had the Colonel for company? And as for the Colonel, well, he wound up being father to an entire country, did he not?

THE SCENT OF REBELLION

The Mansion House was as crowded as the kennel in those days. There was a steady stream of visitors. Some stayed overnight. Others stayed for days and weeks on end, enjoying the hospitality of the Colonel and the Missus. The bedrooms upstairs overflowed. The Colonel loved nothing better than a full house. To sit at a table and dine with friends bubbling over with news and cheer and talk warmed his heart. Still, who could blame him for wanting to get away from the hubbub? He managed to do this daily when, with me at his side, he rode the rounds of his five farms. It was his chance to speak to his overseers, to make sure they were doing their jobs managing the slaves who worked the plantation. He also visited the hogs in their wallow, the sheep in their fold, the cattle in their fields, the chickens in their coop. There was no detail too small for his attention.

More than once, in the woods between farms, I would start a fox. The Colonel would say, "After it, Sweetie!" And, just like that, we would be off, on a foxhunt all our own. Those were some of our jolliest times together, dashing through the woods.

The Colonel often dropped in on his neighbors, particularly the Fairfaxes at Belvoir. Belvoir was a mansion up the river that was even grander than the Colonel's. The Fairfaxes hailed from

England. All of their fine furnishings—which the Colonel so greatly admired—had come from England. The Colonel went there to dine or to play cards—endless rollicking hands of whist and loo. He also liked to keep company with Sally Fairfax, the lady of the house. The Fairfaxes had hounds of their own, who lazed on the porch or by the fireplace. The Colonel kept me from mixing with them, for they often had the mange. They were not fit company for a lady like myself.

Another of his neighbors was George Mason. Sometimes the Colonel visited Mason, and other times he wrote letters to him. The Colonel loved writing letters. He labored hard at the task. I would lie at the Colonel's feet and groom my toes with my tongue as he sat at his desk. The steady scratching sound of the quill feather across the paper often lulled me to sleep. I would awake to the sound of

the Colonel reading aloud the letters he had written. How I loved the sound of his voice!

One day, when I was not much older than one year, he read aloud a letter to George Mason. Something had happened not so long ago to stir the ire of the Colonel. Before this time, he had been a peaceful Virginia planter. But suddenly, he was a firebrand! There had been riots in a city up north called Boston against something called the Townshend Acts. These were laws that taxed paper, paint, glass, lead, and tea. To beat down the rioters, British troops had stormed Boston. Over a year later, the Colonel was still fuming about this as he wrote to Mason.

"At a time when our lordly masters in Great Britain will be satisfied with nothing less than the deprivation of American freedom, it seems highly necessary that something should be done to avert the stroke and maintain the liberty which we have derived from our ancestors. But the manner of doing it to answer the purpose effectually is the point in question."

After he finished reading, he looked at me, one eyebrow cocked. Anything he wrote, just like anything he said, was music to my ears. I lifted my head and looked him full in the eyes. *Well put, Colonel,* said I.

Having spent many hours in the company of the Colonel, I knew that Virginia—where the Mansion House Farm was—and twelve other colonies were ruled by England. I knew that England was a powerful master across a vast body of water. Vast as it was, the English kept a tight leash on the colonies. That leash was now chafing. And *that* a dog could well understand.

In the months and years that followed, we would pay many a visit to Gunston Hall, George Mason's plantation. He lived in a fine brick house, every bit as gracious as the Mansion House and Belvoir. It was filled with the kind of beautiful furniture and objects the Colonel loved. Mr. Mason and his missus had a flock of children. I often frolicked with them in the gardens. Just as often, I would remain with the Colonel as he sat in Mr. Mason's study. There they discussed matters of great human import, such as taxation without representation. Together, the two men composed an agreement, which listed the items Virginians must not buy from England so long as England taxed such items so heavily. The Colonel was all for avoiding the tax by making many things at home. He knew it was possible. Among his slaves and servants were woodworkers, seamstresses, tailors, weavers, coopers, blacksmiths—all manner of craftsmen. What need did he have of English goods when there were people on his own plantation who could make such things as furniture, clothing, barrels, and tools? Others in the colonies ought to have been doing the same, he said.

There came a day, in June of 1773, when the Colonel did not show up for his usual evening visit to the kennel. Unless he was away from the Mansion House, he never missed a visit. The hounds milled about and fretted.

Has he gone away again? Pilot wondered.

Perhaps he has fallen ill, said Lawlor.

Perish the thought! said Lady.

It was late that night when he came for me, as brokenhearted as I have ever seen the man. We walked along the riverbank. The crickets were throbbing in the bushes. I could smell the roses blooming as far away as the gardens on the other side of the Mansion House. The Colonel stood and looked out at the moon glinting on the river. I gazed up at his face. It was wet with tears! I had seen Patsy and the Missus shed tears, but never before the Colonel. I wagged my tail.

What is it? What is it, dear Colonel? How can I help?

"Dear, darling, innocent Patsy!" the Colonel whispered. "She was gone in an instant, Sweetie. Taken away from us!"

What did this mean?

The next day, I sat with him in the parlor. He was writing a letter to his brother-in-law, a frequent guest at the Mansion House. Afterward, he read it aloud, with many a pause and tearful sigh.

"Dear Sir," he read. "It is an easier matter to conceive, than to describe the distress of this family, especially that of the unhappy parent of our dear Patsy Custis, when I inform you that yesterday removed the sweet, innocent girl into a more happy and peaceful abode than any she has met with in the afflicted path she hitherto has trod. She rose from dinner about four o'clock in better health and spirits than she appeared to have been in for some time. Soon after which, she was seized with one of her usual fits and expired in it in less than two minutes without uttering a word, a groan, or scarce a sigh. This sudden and unexpected blow, I scarce need add, has almost reduced my poor wife to the lowest ebb of misery . . ."

Here, then, was the cause of his heartbreak! Patsy, the person who had brought me out of the kennel to visit the world for the first time, was gone from this world, taken by the falling sickness.

Later that night, back in the kennel, I lifted my head and bayed over the loss of my dear and gentle playmate, my tea party hostess.

It was a winter's day in December of that same year when I went with the Colonel over to Gunston Hall. Something was afoot—I could tell by the way he drove his horse to an urgent gallop. When we arrived at the hall, the Colonel leapt off his mount and tossed the reins to a slave. He strode up the front porch and into the center hall, calling out: "Mason! Is it true?"

George Mason, a small, roly-poly man, emerged from his study. "It is all too true," he said.

I followed the two men into the study. Mrs. Mason poured tea while the men discussed the big to-do with the Liberty Boys up in Boston. They had dumped many chests of highly taxed tea into Boston Harbor. Furious, the English masters had sailed in on their warships and closed the port of Boston. No ships were allowed in or out. The port was under siege.

"We have been all but invaded!" said the Colonel, slapping his knee.

"There is no doubt; it is a hostile invasion," George Mason agreed.

"If the government continues to demonstrate such a willful determination to overthrow our rights and liberties," said the Colonel, "we will have no choice but to rise up against it."

This was it, then! As sharp as the scent of a fox, rebellion was in the very air.

The Gloucester Hunting Club

I was six years old when the Colonel was chosen by his fellow Virginians to represent them at a very important meeting. The meeting concerned what was to be done about the Intolerable Acts. These were the cruel and unjust tax laws passed by our English masters across the sea. On a bright September morning, when both the Colonel and I would much rather have been foxhunting, we departed the Mansion House Farm in a fine coach.

With us, dressed in livery, was Will Lee. Two other menservants, Giles and Paris, came along, as did Blueskin, tethered to the back of the coach. I rode inside with the Colonel. He stroked my coat steadily. Occasionally, I glanced out the back at Blueskin, trotting along in our wake. His beautiful gray coat was covered in the dust stirred up by the wheels of the coach and the hooves of the matched pair of bays pulling it.

Only the day before, we had bid farewell to the Fairfaxes, George and Sally. The threat of rebellion had sent them fleeing home to England. They asked the Colonel to sell off their beautiful English furniture and to lease out their mansion. The Colonel was sad to see them go but happy to be able to buy some of the furniture for the Mansion House.

As we sat in the coach, the Colonel said, "The world is fast changing, Sweetie. Nothing is as it was. I fear for what is to come."

If the Colonel was afraid, then so was I. As the coach rumbled along, the countryside gave way to more and more buildings. By the time we arrived in the city of Philadelphia, I was cowering behind the Colonel's legs. The world had changed, indeed! Such a din fell on my ears. I had never seen so many people and horses and buildings and coaches before in one place.

"Courage, Sweetie!" the Colonel told me. "You had best get used to the city. We will be here for the duration."

We stayed at Bevan's Inn and, later, at a series of other establishments where the hosts tolerated canine lodgers. But we spent our days at Carpenters' Hall, in a gathering that called itself the Continental Congress. There, men such as John Adams and Richard Henry Lee and Patrick Henry spoke endlessly, shouting and banging their fists on tables. They spoke of war. Boston, that city in the north in the colony of Massachusetts, was still embroiled with British troops. Would the other twelve colonies rally to support them or let them hang alone?

Through the long days in the hall, the Colonel remained silent. As at the dining table back home, he preferred to listen rather than talk.

When we weren't at Carpenters' Hall, we went to the City Tavern or the Rattlesnake—places where the Colonel ate and drank with friends and fellow delegates. Even then, the Colonel listened more than he spoke. He was quietly weighing everything that was said.

One day, when the Congress was not in session, the Colonel took me out for a long walk. By then, I had gotten used to the noise and the bustle of the city streets. I walked at the Colonel's side. I could not help noticing how people stared at him. Was it his fine clothing? His air of calm? Or perhaps it was his height? He towered over the crowds. Whatever their reasons, I was proud to be at the side of such a fine figure of a man.

We were making our way down Walnut Street when an elegant lady stopped us. She nodded cordially to the Colonel. Then she looked at me and exclaimed, "What a beautiful hound! Why, she is every bit as elegant-looking as her master!"

Warmed by the compliment, I preened.

Thanking her, the Colonel introduced himself. We learned that the lady was Elizabeth Powel, mate of Samuel Powel, the mayor of the city.

"I bred her myself," the Colonel said. "Her name is Sweetlips. I don't mind saying that she is the perfect foxhound."

"Is she *really*?" Mrs. Powel said. "My husband,

the mayor, and his friends chase after foxes whenever they can."

The Colonel was at a loss to see where in this big, noisy city one might find a fox, let alone the space in which to chase it.

Mrs. Powel laughed. "Not here. Across the river in New Jersey at the Gloucester Hunting Club."

"What I would not give to ride out to the hounds!" the Colonel said with a sigh. "Unfortunately, I am engaged in important matters at the Congress."

"Surely you can break away from even important matters in pursuit of pleasure," Mrs. Powel said. "Please come and dine with us tonight, and we shall discuss finding the necessary time for hounds and hunting."

That night, we went to the Powels' elegant home. There were many fat, important men sitting around the table. From the smell of their hands, I could tell that they had hounds of their own back home. They admired me. They also admired the Colonel. They saw in him what I saw: a calm, quiet leader.

After that, the Colonel began to spend less time at inns and more time sitting around dining tables with the wealthy men of Philadelphia.

As it happened, the Congress finished early one day. The Colonel summoned me. We walked to the stables, and he saddled up Blueskin. Then we crossed the river to pay a call on the Gloucester Hunting Club.

Blueskin was skittish. *Who are all these people?*

These are the wealthy men of Philadelphia, and they belong to this hunting club, I explained to him.

We came upon a tangle of hounds in a fenced enclosure next to the stable.

The Colonel looked them over. "Legs too short. Ears too short. Dull-eyed. And look, Sweetie. That one over there has the mange! Steer clear of him."

Grrrrr. Who does he think he is, passing judgment on us? the lead hound said to his pack.

He is the Colonel, I spoke up. *Hero of the Indian Wars, Virginia planter, lover of fine things, delegate to the Continental Congress, and finest horseman and foxhunter in all America.*

The hounds curled their lips.

The club's hunt master came along presently to untangle the hounds and bring them out from behind their fence. I joined them, keeping my distance. Eight men, including the Colonel, mounted their horses. The huntsman raised a horn to his lips and blew. How I loved that sound! We were off!

I noticed right away that the terrain was damp and swampy and lent itself poorly to holding scents. The baffled hounds ran with great purpose after nothing very much as far as I could tell. I hung back, not so far as to get under the hooves of the hunt master's mount, but far enough so that I could think and scent for myself. When I finally caught a faint whiff of fox, I made off in my own direction. The other riders continued to follow the pack, but the Colonel knew better. The Colonel followed me.

After a while, the pack did, too, followed by the other horsemen. The scent grew stronger, and eventually, I trapped the fox in a bush against a wall of rock.

My compliments to the newcomer, said the fox. From the depths of the bush, I could just make out her sharp little nose.

A mere trifle, I said.

The other hounds arrived and threw themselves

onto the ground, exhausted and panting.

"Your hound has not disappointed us, Colonel," said Mr. Powel. "This is the first fox we've raised in months."

"A most sagacious beast," said one rider.

"Super-excellent!" said another.

There was much talk, at the Powels' table that night, of the Colonel's elegant riding and of his superb foxhound. I was too busy nibbling at my marrowbone to pay much mind.

We returned to Carpenters' Hall, where discussions had grown more heated. Word had come down from Massachusetts that the British had tried to seize the colonists' store of gunpowder from a place near Boston. The outraged colonists had agreed to ignore the Intolerable Acts and stop paying taxes to England. The British would most definitely use force. Colonists were advised to arm themselves. The men in the hall shouted over one another. Some felt the Bostonians had gone too far. Others felt they had not gone far enough. In the end, John Adams, himself a son of the north, said, "America will support Massachusetts or perish with her."

On that bold note, the Congress broke up. The Colonel and I were only too happy to return to the Mansion House Farm. But as fate would have it, we would not remain there for long.

THE GENERAL'S DOG

Less than one year later, on a May morning in 1775, the Colonel kissed the Missus farewell, and once again climbed into the fancy coach. I could tell right away that this trip differed from our first one to Philadelphia. For one thing, the Colonel had brought another horse in place of Blueskin, a chestnut stallion named Champion. And his friend Richard Henry Lee came with us. All during the ride, the two men discussed the recent events outside Boston, where blood had been shed. The colonists had taken stands against the British at Lexington and Concord. At Concord, the colonial armies had driven the British back into Boston, where now 9,000 colonial soldiers surrounded them.

"I frankly do not see how they managed to do it," said Lee. "They lack food and clothing and weapons. They are not even professional soldiers."

"Tragic that it has come to this," the Colonel said.

But the people on the roadway felt differently. They were all for fighting the British. When farmers and townspeople caught sight of the Colonel's coach, they tossed their hats into the air and cheered. When we neared Philadelphia, hundreds of cavalrymen rode up and surrounded our coach. They escorted us into the city. A brass band struck

up a march, and we paraded into Philadelphia. How very proud I was to be the Colonel's dog.

On the eve of the first day of the second Congress, Will Lee came into the Colonel's room and laid out his finest military uniform. The Colonel would wear it to every meeting.

For weeks the delegates debated. What was to be done about the situation in Boston? Some argued that it was Boston's battle. Let Boston fight it. Others said that Boston's cause belonged to all. One thing was clear to everyone there: if the troops fighting the British did not soon receive aid, they would lose what little ground they had gained. Should the colonies form an army? And, if so, who should lead it? As soon as the question was posed, I knew the answer. I lifted my head and looked right at the Colonel.

You are the only man fit for the job, I said.

As usual, the Colonel was silent, listening to and weighing all that was said.

It took the delegates almost a month to come to the decision I had already reached. On June 14, they voted. Ten companies of riflemen would be sent to serve as an American continental army for one year. On June 15, the delegates appointed a general "to command all the continental forces raised, or to be raised, for the defense of American liberty."

And so it was decided. The Colonel was now the General: General of the Continental Army. And I, it would seem, was now a general's dog.

Three days it took him to work up the courage to write to the Missus and tell her the news.

"My Dearest"—he read aloud his letter in a soft voice—"I am now set down to write to you on a subject which fills me with inexpressible concern—and this concern is greatly aggravated and increased when I reflect on the uneasiness I know it will give you. It has been determined in Congress that the whole army raised for the defense of the American cause shall be put under my care, and that it is necessary for me to proceed immediately to Boston to take upon me the command of it. You may believe me, my dear, when I assure you, in the most solemn manner, that, so far from seeking this appointment, I have used every endeavor in my power to avoid it, not only from my unwillingness to part with you and the family, but from a consciousness of its being a trust too great for my capacity and that I should enjoy more real happiness and felicity in one month with you, at home, than I have the most distant prospect of reaping abroad, if my stay was to be seven times seven years."

Afterward, he lay down on his bed at the inn. I settled myself on the floor beside him. He placed a hand on my head. Was he happy with his new situation? Nay. The General was troubled and sad. I knew how he felt. Like me, he longed for home. But his country needed him. In his letter, he had promised the Missus that he would be home by the fall. As the fortunes of war would have it, he would be over eight years away from home.

As he prepared to leave the next morning, my

eyes followed him. Would he take me with him? Or would he send me home?

"Of course you will go with me," he said, meeting my anxious look. "Generals from the time of Alexander the Great have always gone to war in the company of their dogs."

In the time before I was born, the General had fought side by side with the British soldiers. He dwelled at length on their smart uniforms, their crisp drills, and their well-oiled guns. It broke his heart that he was never accepted as a member of that army. He knew that the army now under his command was not polished and professional like the British. But he was still shocked at what he saw, when, after many parties and parades along the way, we finally arrived in Massachusetts. This Continental Army of his was a ragtag mob of farmers, tradesmen, old men, and boys. They were muddy and tired and disrespectful and unruly. And the stench! Like dogs in a kennel, they did their business where they lived and ate. Some didn't even have rifles or muskets, but armed themselves with pitchforks and hoes. The General stood in the midst of this mob, tall and clean and elegant. He began at once giving orders.

He demanded that the men rise early every morning, wash themselves, and drill regularly. He made them dig holes for doing their business. He whipped the cowards he was told had run from the last fight. And from among the best and bravest, he chose his officers.

"An army must have a strong body of officers," he explained to his aides.

He wanted the army to be ready for battle. He made sure the soldiers kept their horses saddled at all times.

Poor Champion stood around tacked up, day after day. He had expected to go to Philadelphia for a brief visit, perhaps take part in a foxhunt or two. He never expected to go to war.

I don't like this place, he grumbled to me.

Champion wasn't the only grumbler. The soldiers grumbled, too. They didn't like taking orders from a fancy Virginia planter. But the General wanted to take Boston back from the British, and that is what he intended to do.

The General made his headquarters in a large house in Cambridge. The Missus soon joined him, as she would every year of the war. I could tell that the noise of the cannons and shells put her off. But she did her best to remain brave and cheerful. Many were the evenings when the General and the Missus would sit by the fire, every bit as cozily as if they were back home at the Mansion House Farm.

The Missus would knit socks for the soldiers. The General would stretch out his long legs before him. His eyes were closed, but from my place on the floor tiles, I could see him thinking. Planning. Plotting. You might wonder why a dog came to know so much about military matters. Well, I was a general's dog, steeped in the business of war. These eyes saw things done. These ears pricked up at things said. One way or another, I knew what was going on.

On the night of March 4, 1776, the General ordered his men to load up every wagon with sticks and logs. Then he had them wrap boots, horses' hooves, and wagon wheels in straw and cloth. It was not until we got under way that I understood. He was muffling their sounds. As quietly as cats, we moved down to the place on Boston Harbor called Dorchester Neck. There, under cover of darkness, within firing distance of the British on the other shore, the soldiers built ramparts. When the soldiers' work was done, the General sent them back to the camp and ordered down a fresh group to man the ramparts. By the light of the rising sun, the British beheld the Continental Army just across the water. Imagine the look of surprise on their faces! The patriots raised their guns and prepared to fire.

The British were getting ready to return fire, when a great, dark storm cloud swept in from the north. The sky turned black as pitch. The heavens opened, and down came a drenching torrent of rain. The British fled. They piled onto their ships and sailed out of Boston Harbor that very day. And—just like that!—Boston was back in American hands. The Battle of Dorchester Heights was the General's first victory.

THE DARKEST HOUR

When I would return to the Mansion House Farm many years later, the dogs all came sniffing after me.

You smell like gunpowder, some said.

You smell like blood and death, others said.

They all wanted to know what it was like to be in the war.

The fact was it wasn't all cannons and pikes and bayonets. As in much of life, it was mostly rather humdrum. There were the usual daily drills and housekeeping tasks the General put to the men. But then there were vast stretches of idle time. They passed it by playing cards and other games. Their most strenuous game was Find the Cannonball. Day after day, to show their might, the British fired cannonballs over enemy lines. Our men held contests to see who could find and retrieve the most cannonballs. Many times I yelped and leapt aside as a gang came hurtling after a rolling cannonball. In their careless need for exercise and amusement, how they reminded me of my brothers back at the kennel!

Meanwhile, the General was engaged in more serious matters, such as the fact that there were never enough rifles, nor powder, nor soldiers, nor uniforms, nor food. Every night, before the General lay down on his cot to sleep, he would take out his field desk and write letters. He wrote letters to the Congress in Philadelphia, requesting more guns, more powder, more men, more uniforms, more food. He wrote letters to his family and his friends, despairing of his chances of winning a war with an army of ragged bunglers. He went to sleep, discouraged and heavyhearted. But every morning, Will Lee helped him don his uniform. And so, he faced the day, his back ramrod straight, ready to do the best he could with what little he had. I had always admired the man. But never more so than in those dark days.

Following our victory in Boston, we decamped south to New York. The British had fled Boston. But they could not afford to let the Americans hold the valuable port of New York. When the British returned to New York, the General and his army would be waiting for them. The General ordered the soldiers to build a fort on Long Island in the hills of Brooklyn Heights. From there, they would be able to protect the entrance to the Hudson River and keep the British out. The soldiers stood sentry and watched and waited for General Howe and his British troops to come. Then, one morning in late August, sails appeared on the horizon. By the end of the day, there were thirty enemy ships filling the harbor. The days of waiting were over.

The British wasted no time. They gave the Americans a good drubbing at a place called Gowanus Pass. Then they circled around the patriots' backs. British soldiers, marching steadily, drove the Americans all the way back to their fort. From behind the mud and log ramparts, the patriot army stared with frightened eyes at row upon row of British soldiers, rifles at the ready. They knew they were done for. But much to the General's surprise, the British did not storm the fort. Shouldering their rifles, they swung around and marched away.

When the British returned to capture the soldiers, they found the fort empty. Every last soldier had slipped through the woods and down to the riverbank. There, the General had lined up all the boats he could muster. Under cover of night, he ferried the soldiers across the river to safety in Manhattan. While the General had saved his men, there was no doubt that the British had won the Battle of Long Island.

Two weeks later, on the island of Manhattan, five warships dropped anchor offshore and began firing their cannons at the small band of patriot soldiers hunkered down in shallow trenches. These soldiers were farm boys with little experience of, and less taste for, battle. One look at the soldiers rowing ashore in long barges, and those boys abandoned their trenches and ran for their lives.

I was with the General when we heard the thundering of the British cannons. Where most men would have run away, the General spurred his horse and charged toward that fearful booming. We soon met up with the men fleeing the enemy. Bloody and wild-eyed, they streamed past the General.

"Stay put, men! Stand your ground!" the General shouted to them.

But they only ran faster.

Two fresh brigades arrived. The General ordered them to shelter behind a stone wall and make their stand. But when the columns of British soldiers marched into view, our boys threw down their guns and beat a hasty retreat.

The General was beside himself. He shouted at them. He swatted them with his riding crop. In disgust, he flung his hat down on the ground and cried, "Are these the men with whom I am to defend America?"

I stared up at him. The General had a temper, but he usually kept it in check. And now, the enemy was fast approaching! I howled, *General, we must run away! It's not safe for us to stay here!*

But he did not heed me. So despairing was he at this moment, I believe the General actually wanted the enemy to take him.

In the nick of time, Will and two of the General's aides came galloping onto the scene. They spoke to him in urgent whispers. Finally, all four men wheeled around and ran. I picked up the General's hat in my mouth and followed them back to Fort Washington. I might not have been bred to retrieve, but I could not leave the General's hat lying there in the dust for the enemy to tread on.

So went the Battle of Kip's Bay, a bitter defeat for the Continental Army.

The following day, a scout patrol ran into British troops hiding in some rocky woods not far from Fort Washington in Harlem Heights. The British marched out into the open and attacked. But the Americans hid behind the rocks and trees and held their ground. This time it was the British who ran away. The General declared the Battle of Harlem

Heights a victory for the Continental Army.

Just as the General was a listener instead of a talker, in times of war, he was a watcher more than a doer. For weeks, he watched from the stony heights as General Howe prepared his next move. On October 12, British ships sailed up the East River into Long Island Sound. Washington was not happy. He feared that the British would head up the coast and block the Continental Army from entering New England. At top speed, he marched his troops up to White Plains, just north of where British ships had landed. On some hills, he had the men build battlements. I sniffed at them doubtfully. They were flimsy things, made of nothing more than dead cornstalks and mud.

"We work with what we have, Sweetlips," the General said with a weary sigh.

We took up a post on a high hill and made

ready for battle. When the British marched in, they rapidly captured a hill nearby, all too close to us. That night, the General ordered us to decamp to a higher hill. But the next day, the British turned and made away, in the direction of the Hudson River.

What was General Howe up to now? Over breakfast, my general discussed this with his officers. Was Howe sending his troops farther north to block us from entering New England? Or were they crossing the Hudson River into New Jersey and, from there, marching southeast to take Philadelphia? Allowing for all possibilities, the General decided to leave some troops behind, under General Charles Lee. They would defend the American position in New England. Meanwhile, my general would cross the Hudson and gather New Jersey troops to defend Philadelphia. He had wanted to evacuate Fort Washington, the one remaining American foothold in New York. But Congress insisted he hold on to it. Reluctantly, he left troops there, under Colonel Magaw. Across the river, he kept more troops at Fort Lee, New Jersey, under General Nathanael Greene, to prevent the British from sailing up the Hudson. Fort Washington, he hoped, would be safe. It was a large and sprawling fortification. Besides, the British would no more storm it than they had the fort at Brooklyn Heights. As long as Fort Washington stood, Fort Lee would hold. Or so the General prayed.

We were on the road to Philadelphia when we got the news. A rider came galloping after us.

"The British are advancing on Fort Washington!" he reported breathlessly.

The General had not had a day's rest since we left Philadelphia for Boston over a year earlier.

He was exhausted and deeply discouraged. Yet he whipped around and charged back to Fort Lee.

Alas, too late! I stood with the General, on the banks of the Hudson River. We watched the British forces bear down on three sides of Fort Washington. The men holed up inside knew they were outnumbered and outsmarted. They surrendered. As the sun sank, so did our hearts. The British flag now waved over the ramparts of Fort Washington. Standing with us on the riverbank was a man named Thomas Paine. His had been one of the loudest voices in favor of the revolt. And now he saw the revolt unraveling.

There was no time to rue the defeat at Fort Washington. The General rushed to clear out of Fort Lee and take valuable stores with him. He knew there wasn't much time. Three days after Fort Washington fell, the British crossed the river

and marched upon Fort Lee. There was nothing for us to do but leave. Taking what little we could carry, we fled farther into New Jersey.

Now I knew how it felt to be a fox pursued by baying dogs. The British hounded us every step of the way across New Jersey. Our troops were exhausted, the officers were in a panic, and the flat land offered no rocks or trees for cover. The General did everything he could to keep the army moving and out of range of enemy fire. The towns we passed through were disheartened by the sight of the fleeing patriots. They prepared themselves to surrender to the British.

When Congress got word of the many defeats in New York, they began to lose faith in the General. It was enough to make even a general's dog like me drop to the ground and give up.

THE DOGS OF WAR

Winter had fallen. It was dark and gloomy and cold. The General spent many a night wrapped in his greatcoat, sitting around the campfire with his aides and officers. Whenever I smell wet wool drying in the heat of a wood fire, my thoughts drift back to those days. The General used those firelit nights to ponder his next move against the enemy. Luckily for us, General Howe was not fond of winter fighting. His armies had gone to camps in the north to wait out the winter. But he had left army posts behind all over New Jersey. The General wanted the British out of New Jersey. He planned to attack those posts.

There was one post across the river in Trenton that the General had his sights fixed on. It was manned by German soldiers-for-hire fighting for the British. They were called Hessians—a name like a hissing tomcat—and they were every bit as scrappy and fierce. But the General was not afraid. To restore the confidence of all, the General needed a victory badly.

On the night before the attack, the General stood before his men and read aloud from a writing of Thomas Paine:

"These are the times that try men's souls: The summer soldier and the sunshine patriot will, in this crisis, shrink from the service of their country;

but he that stands it now, deserves the love and thanks of man and woman. Tyranny . . . is not easily conquered; yet we have this consolation with us, that the harder the conflict, the more glorious the triumph."

The General then marched 2,400 men, warmed by these words, behind the hills along the Delaware. In big boats pushed by men with long poles, the Continental Army set off across the river. Sharp pieces of ice, like smashed crockery, floated everywhere. Even worse, as my twitching whiskers told me, a storm was in the offing!

The other dogs among us fretted. Have I said that I was not the only dog in the Continental Army? Many officers, like the General, had brought their dogs with them from home. There was also a large band of homeless strays that followed the army, looking for food and companionship. This river, churning and groaning with ice, was no place for pet or stray or even water dog. Many dogs whimpered and refused to cross. I knew I had to act.

Some of them I merely had to nudge onto the boats. Others I chased and herded. There was one stubborn and frightened little spaniel whose ears I was forced to nip. *Quickly now, and don't hold us back,* I urged him. *If we strike before sunrise, we will have the advantage.*

One after another, the frightened and reluctant dogs boarded the boats.

After several boatloads of men and dogs had crossed, the wind began to build. The next boat loaded up and departed. Freezing water slapped against the sides and drenched the men. The river ice thickened so that the men had trouble finding the bottom with their poles. The next boat was ready to board.

"You make this crossing, Sweetie," the General said to me.

I did not want to. This boat was filled with horses. A single panicked horse could sink a boat such as this.

The General said to me, "Come now, Sweetie. Show me the courage you have inspired in these other dogs."

I gave him my most soulful look. *Can't I cross later with you?* I asked.

"Go now, Sweetlips," the General said.

I knew my orders when I heard them. I gathered my courage and leapt aboard. The deck tilted, slick with ice, as the boat crossed the river. The horses slipped and slid, their eyes rolling. They shrieked and lunged. Frantically, I scrambled to avoid getting crushed beneath their icy hooves or kicked overboard into the river. When the boat

butted against the far bank, I leapt ashore, shook the ice off my coat, and let out a loud sneeze of pure relief.

The crossing of the boats took longer than the General had expected. His plan to attack before dawn, like so many of his plans in this war, was dashed.

One of the General's aides said to him, "It's a nine-mile slog to the Hessian camp. The snow's getting deeper all the time. The men will never make it."

"The men will have to make it," the General said steadily. "They must."

The storm was upon us full force now. Sleet fell in icy sheets. If the sun had risen, I did not see it for the shroud of dark clouds that hung overhead. I have never felt such cold! But I was covered in fur. The men weren't so lucky. Some of them had holes in their boots and left bloody footprints in the snow.

As the Hessians slept peacefully in their snow-shrouded huts, we surrounded them. When they awoke that Christmas Day, their surprise was complete. Blinded by snow, many Hessians met their doom that morning. But the Continental Army lost not a single man. The Battle of Trenton was a victory for the Americans.

We continued our raids throughout New Jersey, stopping to rest at Morristown Heights. The nights were cold, and the campfires drew the dogs out from the shadows. Like the General, I was not born with the gift of gab. Some of these dogs were right chatterboxes. As I lay bathed in the fire's warmth, tending to my war-weary feet, I listened.

A hulking mastiff claimed his place near the fire, unseating a dozing spaniel.

Move aside, runt, and let a real soldier have at that warmth, he growled. *I guard the camp at night and catch enemy spies. What do you do? Sit prettily on your master's lap and drool?*

The spaniel spoke up. *Just because I'm small doesn't mean I'm not a war dog, too.*

The mastiff sneered. *War dog? Parlor dog is more like it!*

I'm not ashamed to admit that I travel slung across

my master's saddle rather than loping alongside the wagon like you, said the spaniel. *But when my master fell in battle, who do you think licked his wound until the doctor could tend to it? Who do you think slept at his side and comforted him when he cried out with fever?*

The mastiff, at a loss for words, merely sniffed.

Then another dog spoke up, this one a ragged mutt. *What about me?* he said. *I'm just a stray. They call me a turnspit dog because I hang around the campfires licking the juice that drips from the roasting meat. A homesick boy soldier from Concord, Massachusetts, found me and adopted me. Now he tells me he writes home to tell his family that I'll be returning with him after the war. He thinks I'm good luck. True, I'm just a flea-bitten mutt, but I'm a war dog, same as you.*

Then the good-luck mutt turned to me. *What*

about you? A battlefield's no place for a dainty lass like yourself.

How dare you? The mastiff reared up. *Anyone with any sense knows she's the General's dog. Where he goes, she goes. She runs beside his horse and sleeps beneath his cot and listens to his every plan. You are not fit to sniff her tail.*

The spaniel and several other dogs yipped and growled in agreement.

I spoke up at last. *Now, now, fellows,* I said. *All of us here serve a purpose. There's no need to fight. May I remind you that we are all on the same side in this battle?*

Spoken like a true general's dog, said the spaniel. *Why, without your encouragement, I would never have gotten across the icy river on that boat. Just like our General, you give us hope and heart.*

Hear, hear! the dogs all cheered.

Suddenly, all eyes were on me.

I was so overcome with emotion that I quickly returned to the business of grooming my feet.

It was about this time that I had the pleasure of meeting one of the General's greatest admirers: the Frenchman Lafayette.

I had never known a Frenchman until then. There had been talk of the French around many a camp table and fire. The French were enemies of the British. And now they had decided to help the Continental Army rid America of their common enemy. They sent money and weapons and officers to advise. Lafayette was one such officer.

Although the Congress had given him the rank of Major General, this Lafayette was just a pup. I liked him. In his elegance and polish, he reminded me of the General. But the Frenchman had a great deal to learn about war. Luckily for him, the General was a good teacher. Lafayette also showered a great deal of attention on me. That gentleman was quite the flirt, bringing me small treats from the table and stroking my coat. At first, I thought it was because I was the General's dog. You would be surprised how many of the General's officers attempted to curry favor with the General by making a fuss over me. I saw through this and usually put my nose up. But Lafayette was different. He paid attention to me because he loved dogs. He had trained dogs and hunted with them in his far-off land of France. He knew how to ask me to sit, stay, and come. Although the words he used were different, I could tell what he wanted by his tone and his hands. He wanted what any man wants of a dog: to sit, to stay, to come.

"Ah, *ma chère* Sweetlips!" he crooned to me. "If only I could get you together with the hounds in my kennel. *Les chiens normands.* They are fine, big dogs and so skillful at the hunting! They hunt the stag and the boar and can follow a three-days-old trail! How they would worship you, my sleek, beautiful American foxhound!"

PRISONER OF WAR

It was June when the General's army, exhausted from the long march south, took a stand on the far side of the Brandywine River near Philadelphia. But General Howe's army sneaked up behind us. The General ordered the rear guard to turn and fight while the rest of the Continental Army sought to escape. The British pursued us. Howe attempted to drive us out into the open for a British-style battle. But this the General would not allow. He kept his soldiers out of firing range. And, while he did that, unfortunately, Howe busied himself capturing Philadelphia for the British.

Philadelphia, the city where the Continental Congress had met, the very seat of American liberty, fell to the British! But, still, the General was not to be discouraged.

In the dead of night, on October 3, 1777, the General's armies moved in stealth toward British troops encamped at Germantown, near Philadelphia. It was a sneak attack, just like the one the General had led in Trenton. Instead of a snowstorm to hide us, there was now a thickening fog. At first, the General gave thanks, for the fog hid his armies. But once fighting broke out, the fog hampered it. Unable to see beyond the ends of their own rifles, the patriots could not tell friend from foe. They fired blindly into the fog. The British ran around, carrying torches. As they retreated, they set fire to mills and fields. Acrid smoke, adding to fog, choked us. The British gave us a thorough trouncing.

In the confusion, I lost sight of the General. Some of the British troops had taken cover in a big stone house. The patriots surrounded it and attacked. The British fired their muskets from every window. Many patriots fell laying siege to that house. Dodging gunfire, I scrambled about among the soldiers. Where was the General? But the smoke and gunpowder played tricks with my nose. I was completely befuddled. Oh, how I hated war at that moment! I was so weary of marching and camping and fighting! I longed for the warmth and familiarity of the Mansion House Farm.

That was when I came upon a certain little brown dog.

Aha! he said as he trotted up to me through the fog. *I thought I smelled a female lurking somewhere about.*

He sported a smart leather collar.

This fog is a right menace, eh, what? said the brown dog.

I was unfamiliar with this dog. He wasn't one of ours. I could see that he was well-fed and nicely groomed. He was no turnspit dog. This was a gentleperson's dog if ever I saw one. A lapdog.

I sniffed at him, and then bristled. This one sat in the lap of the enemy!

Who are you? I growled. *Reveal yourself!*

With pride. I'm the General's dog, he said.

Begging your pardon, but I *am the General's dog,* I replied haughtily.

We're both Generals' dogs, then. So much the better, he said, *for we can be friends.*

On the contrary, I said, pulling myself up to my full height, *we are sworn enemies!*

Tut-tut, said the dog coolly. *Men have their reasons for doing battle. That doesn't mean we dogs have to share them.* He nuzzled me.

It was then that one of the General's aides came upon us.

"Sweetlips! What are you doing wandering around? Haven't you heard? We are in full retreat. And who, pray tell, is this furry scamp?"

The aide picked up the little dog. He read the metal plate on his collar. His jaw dropped. "The

119

General will want to see this right away. Come along, Sweetie. It looks like you've captured yourself a prisoner of war."

I followed the aide as he marched through the fog with the little dog.

The soldiers we passed peered curiously at him.

"Sweetlips has nabbed General Howe's dog!" the aide said.

"You don't say," one of the soldiers said. "What are you going to do with him? Roast him on a spit?"

"I was thinking he would make a splendid mascot," the aide said. "Or perhaps we might ransom him for a tidy sum?"

"Capital ideas, both!" another soldier said.

"Let's see what the General has to say," the aide replied.

By the time we caught up with the General, a small band of soldiers were marching in our wake.

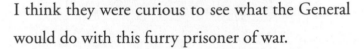

I think they were curious to see what the General would do with this furry prisoner of war.

It was Will who saw me first. "Sweetlips!" he cried. "Where have you been? The General's been worried sick about you."

I wagged my tail. How nice it was to be missed!

The General's face lit up when he saw me. "Sweetlips! I feared you had been caught in the crossfire." Then he looked at the soldiers. Many were wounded and downcast.

"Don't be dispirited!" the General said. "You

held your own well against the flower of the British army. While it is unfortunate that we did not win, neither did we lose all that badly."

Hearing this, the soldiers appeared to stand a little taller. The General always knew how to buck up their sagging spirits. Suddenly, his eye fell on the little dog. He raised a brow.

"You'll never guess what Sweetlips has found," the aide said eagerly. "None other than the pet dog of General Howe."

The General held out his arms for the dog. His long pale fingers combed the animal's fur for mange and checked his ears for ticks. "He seems none the worse for wear," he said, holding the little dog high in the air. "Blundered behind enemy lines, did you, little fellow?"

The little brown dog cut me a look. *So this is your general?*

The finest there is, I replied.

The General handed off the dog to an aide. He ordered the dog to be washed and brushed and fed.

Your general is a gentleman of the first order, the little dog said as they bore him off to his bath.

Later, to the great disappointment of many of the men, the General returned the dog to his British master. One of his aides wrote a note to Howe, which he read aloud to the General before sending it along with the dog to enemy headquarters.

"General Washington's compliments to General Howe. He does himself the pleasure to return to him a dog, which accidentally fell into his hands, and by the inscription on the collar appears to belong to General Howe."

That was my general! A man who could suffer defeat at his enemy's hands one moment and, the next, return a stray dog to him.

10

HONORABLE DISCHARGE

While the British spent that winter in warmth
and comfort in the captured city of Philadelphia,
the Continental Army suffered bitterly in our
camp at Valley Forge. Not the least of the suffer-
ers was yours truly. The war had taken its toll on
me. My bones ached and my ribs showed, and I
moved more slowly those days. The men, cold and
ragged, were even worse off. The General, as usual,
seemed untouched by misfortune. He ordered the

men to build shelters. They made fireplaces in the huts with mud over lath. They burned every stick of wood they could lay hands on staying warm. There was little forage for the horses and, sadly, many died. The surrounding farms had sold most of their food to the British, and what little food the men scrounged was not fit for a dog's bowl. Many were the nights I put my nose up at their scraps.

I do not know when things began to look up. Perhaps it was when the Missus arrived in her coach. Life was always brighter when she was at hand. But it might have been when the German who called himself von Steuben joined us along with his greyhound, Azor.

The German did not speak the language. He spoke the language of drills. In no time at all, he had that ragged bunch of soldiers marching and wielding their rifles as smartly as British soldiers.

I stood beside Azor and reviewed the troops.

This pitiful army would be nothing without my master, Azor said.

Begging your pardon, my needle-nosed friend, I said, *but this pitiful army has won many a battle and will go on to win many more—with or without your master.* Whether this was true, I knew not. But someone had to stand up for our boys.

As the army improved the drill, so did our boys' spirits lift. Soon, the campground rang with the sound of singing and rowdy games.

The news came that the French were joining the war on the side of the patriots. On May 5, 1778, the soldiers passed before the General and his staff and guests of honor from France. They lined up in their ranks and shouted, "Huzzah! Long live the king of France." They were a pretty sight. I have never seen the General more pleased and proud.

That evening, as he sat with the Missus by the fire, he spoke with great optimism about the war, now that the French were with us. We finally had a chance of winning. As he wrote in his letter to Congress, "I believe no event was ever received with more heartfelt joy." Now there would be more soldiers, more weapons, more powder, more uniforms, more food. No longer would the Continental Army be the underdog.

I dozed by the fire, very nearly as contented as the General.

The Missus lowered her knitting. "As for me, Old Man," she said—for that was her pet name for him—"I know that I leave you this year with a heart far less heavy than last."

"I am glad," said the General. After a brief silence, he said, "Will you do me a kindness? Take my dear Sweetie back home with you."

I lifted my head from my paws. Had someone spoken my name?

"She'll be ten years old this year," the General was saying. "She isn't as fast as she once was. Why, I nearly lost her in the last skirmish. My obligations force me to remain. While I have grown gray in the service of my country, it is unfair to ask the same of this faithful hound."

"If that is your wish, Old Man," said the Missus, "I will return her to the kennel."

"I would much prefer that you give her the run of the house," the General said. "She has earned the privilege."

The next day, I climbed into the coach with the Missus.

I looked out at him. *You cannot be serious!*

"Sweetlips, consider yourself honorably discharged from the Continental Army."

Then the General wished us God's speed.

"Watch over the Missus," he told me.

I will, I said, licking his hand. *But who will watch over you, good sir?*

Then he thumped the roof of the coach, and the team surged forward.

The General stood waving. Long after the Missus had turned around, I kept watch out the back window. The General's form, so tall and straight and dear to me, grew smaller and smaller. My tail wagged slower and slower. Would I ever see the General again?

And so the General and I went our separate ways: he off to claim more victories, me home to the Mansion House Farm. How I would miss him, for I would see him only twice during the next five years. Once when he passed through Virginia on his way to victory at the Battle of Yorktown. The second time, not long after the first, following the death and burial of Jacky, his stepson. Jacky had gone with him to Yorktown as his aide and had died there of sickness. The Missus, once again, was undone by the loss of a child. But two grandchildren remained to fill the halls of the Mansion House with their happy cries.

For much of the remainder of the war, the Missus stayed at the General's side. Life at the house was not the same without the General walking the halls, poking the embers, scratching out letters with his feather quill. Lund Washington managed the property while his cousin was away at war. He did his best to look after things, but he was not the General. The house had fallen into frightful disrepair, and the gardens were a shambles.

Lund did not neglect me, I am happy to say. When he saw that I was most comfortable in the parlor, he made sure there was always a fire in the grate. Every time I heard the front door open, I would look up eagerly, expecting the General to walk in. But it was usually Lund, or one of the neighbors. They often sat in the parlor and spoke of the war and of the many battles I was missing.

The General did not come home for good until two years after the Battle of Yorktown, when a peace treaty was signed. I heard the *clip-clop* of horses' hooves approaching. I made my way slowly to the front of the house and peered through the window glass. I was fifteen years old and nearly blind, but I could make out the familiar outline of his tall, elegant form riding side by side with the faithful Will Lee. How weary and careworn they both looked!

The Missus, who was at home at the time, rushed in from the dining room. With a joyful cry, she flung open the front door. Leaving the couple to their happy reunion, I retreated to my place by the parlor fire. I knew the General would know where to find me.

I must have fallen into a doze, for I awoke to the sound of a voice I would have known anywhere.

"Sweetie!" he said. "You waited for me."

Of course I waited for you! Whatever took you so long?

In the days that followed, joints creaking, I went with the General on his rounds. Now that I had him back, I would not let him out of my sight. Luckily for my old bones, he spent a good deal of his time near the fire, writing to his friends. He wrote to Lafayette: "At length my dear Marquis I am becoming a private citizen on the banks of the Potomac, and under the shadow of my own vine and my own fig tree." To another friend he wrote of the time of peace and quiet that awaited him now that the war was over. He intended to spend that time "cultivating the affections of good men and in the practice of the domestic virtues . . . as I travel gently down the stream of life until I sleep with my fathers."

As it turned out, before he would sleep, the General's country would call upon him again, this time to lead them as its first president. I would not live to see that day. By then, I had gone to sleep with my own furry fathers. But I passed on from this world knowing that the General would continue to serve his country with loyalty and steadfastness, just as I, the perfect foxhound, had served the General, in times of war and peace. And this much I can tell you: a more fortunate dog there never was.

APPENDIX

More About George Washington

Everyone knows that George Washington is the father of his country. But the American Kennel Club credits him as the father of the American foxhound as well.

Washington loved hunting foxes at his Virginia homestead, Mount Vernon, which he called the Mansion House Farm. As his step-grandson, George Washington Parke Custis, wrote in his memoirs: "There were roads cut through the woods in various directions, by which aged and timid hunters and ladies could enjoy the exhilarating cry, without risk of life or limb; but Washington rode gaily up to his dogs, through all the difficulties and dangers of the ground on which he hunted, nor spared his generous steed, as the distended nostrils of Blueskin often would show."

Washington loved dogs. Over the years, he owned all kinds, from lapdogs to herders to coach dogs, which was what Dalmatians were called in those days. As an avid foxhunter, he had enormous enthusiasm for hunting hounds. This much is obvious from the vivid and original names he gave them: Venus, Truelove, Taster, Juno, True Man, Music. According to psychologist and animal writer Stanley Coren, in his delightful book *The Pawprints of History,* one of Washington's favorites was Sweetlips, the "perfect foxhound." According to Coren, Sweetlips accompanied her master to the Constitutional Convention in Philadelphia. There, she and George met Elizabeth Powel, wife of the mayor, who admired Washington's handsome fox-hound almost as much as she did the dog's master. It was through Elizabeth that Washington met some of the most prominent men of Philadelphia, whom he dined with and, on occasion, went fox-hunting with at a club across the river in Trenton, New Jersey.

Coren playfully suggests that since these powerful men would later support George Washington's promotion to commander of the Continental forces, Sweetlips had a modest "paw" in her master's success. It is not much of a stretch to place Sweetlips at Washington's side in the Revolutionary War since he did not return home after the convention, and it was not unheard of for soldiers to bring their dogs with them to war.

Sweetlips probably bore a closer resemblance to an English foxhound than to today's American foxhound. That was because Washington had not yet introduced into his kennel a strain of French hound. How do people today know so much about Washington and his dogs? In his private papers, Washington took careful notes about what went on in his kennel: which dogs he was breeding, when dogs had whelped, and the names and descriptions of the pups. He also recorded when they were doused for mange and rabies (using his own homemade remedies), neutered, or locked away in the barn so they would not get pregnant. Despite his careful planning, however, many times his dogs chose their own mates, rather than the ones he had picked for them.

During the Revolutionary War, Washington made fast friends with the Marquis de Lafayette, himself a hunter and dog lover. Lafayette spoke glowingly of the many types of French hunting hounds. After the war, in 1785, Lafayette arranged to have his friend Count Doilliamson ship seven hounds from France as a gift to Washington. The hounds traveled in the company of John Quincy Adams, who was returning from a posting in Paris. No dog lover, Adams was so eager to get home to Massachusetts that he left the poor hounds stranded in a warehouse on the docks of New York. Piqued, Washington was able to arrange for the dogs' shipment to Virginia.

Interestingly, while many believe these hounds to have been blue Gascons, the current Count Doilliamson maintains that they were *chiens normands,* or Normandy hounds. Perhaps that is why these hounds were such a disappointment as fox-hunters. Still, Washington was able to breed them with excellent results. The French hounds were noisy, with a bay as loud as "the bells of Moscow."

And they were large. Custis recalls how he and the other children used to ride upon the backs of these brutes as if they were horses. One hound in particular loomed large in his recollections. His name was Vulcan—not the same Vulcan who was Sweetlips's littermate, but another genuine character.

As Custis tells it: "It happened that upon a large company sitting down to dinner at Mount Vernon one day, the lady of the mansion (my grandmother) discovered that the ham, the pride of every Virginia housewife's table, was missing from its accustomed post of honor. Upon questioning Frank, the butler, this portly, and at the same time the most polite and accomplished of all butlers, observed that a ham—yes, a very fine ham—had been prepared, agreeably to the madam's orders, but lo and behold! who should come into the kitchen, while the savory ham was smoking in its dish, but old Vulcan, the hound, and without more ado fastened his fangs into it; and although they of the kitchen had stood to such arms as they could get, and had fought the old spoiler desperately, yet Vulcan had finally triumphed, and bore off the prize, ay, 'cleanly, under the keeper's nose.' The lady by no means relished the loss of a dish that formed the pride of her table, and uttered some remarks by no means favorable to old Vulcan, or indeed to dogs in general, while the chief [Washington], having heard the story, communicated it to his guests, and, with them, laughed heartily at the exploit of the staghound."

While Washington continued to breed dogs after the war, his foxhunting days were numbered. Where once he had gone out two to three times a week during the season, now he was reduced to two or three times a year. Why was this so? Perhaps it was because he was getting on in years, and eight years of war had taken their toll. Foxhunting, especially as Washington practiced it, was a rigorous and even dangerous sport. Or perhaps he had simply moved on to other interests, such as the design and construction of a vast deer park on the property. Whatever the reason, his last foxhunt took place on February 15, 1788, when he was nearing the age of fifty-six. As he recorded in his papers, "Let out a fox (which had been taken alive some days ago) and after chasing it an hour lost it." By the time he left Mount Vernon to serve as the first president of the United States, he had disbanded his kennel and given away most of his hounds.

The war had also brought about another big change in Washington. Before he left Mount Vernon to head up the Continental Army, he was a typical Virginia planter. He supported slavery as an institution that had existed for thousands of years, viewing it as a simple fact of life. Washington had first become a slave owner at the age of eleven, when his father died and left him ten slaves. Through inheritance, the birth of new children, and the purchase of more than sixty people, the enslaved population at Mount Vernon grew steadily up until the revolution. During the war, Washington became morally opposed to slavery.

By 1778, he no longer wanted to own slaves and decided that it was wrong to break up family groups on the auction block.

What had caused this change? Perhaps it was the years spent fighting for the principle of freedom. Perhaps it was seeing black soldiers fighting for the cause of liberty alongside white soldiers in his army (about 20 percent of Washington's army was African American). Perhaps it was the time he spent with fellow officers like Alexander Hamilton or the Marquis de Lafayette or John Laurens from South Carolina, to whom slavery was an out-and-out evil.

Washington believed that the best way to abolish slavery was through legislation. But as president, he felt that the time was not right for such a change. The conflict that would have arisen between North and South would have torn apart the nation in its infancy.

In spite of this, Washington took steps to back up his own beliefs with action. In his will, he said that Will Lee should be freed immediately and left him an annual payment. Until the end of his days, Will Lee worked as a cobbler at Mount Vernon, where many veterans of the revolution would stop by and pay their respects.

Freeing the rest of the slaves was a more complex

matter. Of all the Mount Vernon slaves, less than half belonged to George and many more—known as "dower slaves"—belonged to the descendants of Martha's first husband, Daniel Parke Custis. Freeing the dower slaves would require getting the permission of the Custis heirs, who would also want to be paid for the value of those slaves. Washington tried to sell his western lands in order to have the money to make that payment, but no one would purchase his land. Another complication was that many of Washington's slaves had intermarried with the dower slaves.

Washington directed in his will that, following the death of Martha, all the Mount Vernon slaves who belonged to him—about 123 men, women, and children—were to be freed. By law, the dower slaves—roughly 153 people—would be divided among Mrs. Washington's four Custis grandchildren. This meant that many families, where one parent belonged to George Washington and the other to the Custis family, were torn apart. It is important to note that George Washington was the only slave-owning president to free all of his slaves.

For more information about George Washington, visit the excellent website maintained by Mount Vernon:

- mountvernon.org/georgewashington

For more on dogs at Mount Vernon, check out:

- mountvernon.org/educational-resources /encyclopedia/dogs-mount-vernon

Now you can read the actual papers of George Washington online at the Library of Congress!

- memory.loc.gov/ammem/gwhtml/gwhome .html

The History of the American Foxhound

On June 30, 1650, an Englishman named Robert Brooke arrived in what is now Calvert County in southern Maryland, introducing the first pack of English foxhounds to the colonies. In America, they were bred to run with horses and to track their quarry, usually the gray fox, across the rugged terrain of the South. In 1814, the Duke of Leeds gave two Irish foxhounds, Mountain and Muse, to his guest Bolton Jackson. These hounds were eventually bred with the descendants of Brooke's dogs, forming the main background for the American foxhound, first recognized as a breed by the American Kennel Club in 1886.

The American Foxhound Today

Bred to be lighter, faster, and taller than the English foxhound, the American foxhound is long-legged, measuring anywhere from twenty-two to twenty-eight inches tall at the shoulder. With its broad, hanging ears and its upward-curving tail, it looks a little like a beagle on stilts. Its shorthaired coat comes in any number of color combinations— red, brown, black, white. Some types of American hound are entered into competitive field trials, where speed counts. Others are used for the sport of foxhunting, where slower, more careful tracking and scenting come into play. (Readers will be happy to know that foxhunting in America today, unlike in Washington's time, does not involve the killing of the fox!) Still others are pack hounds, used by hunters and farmers.

Owning an American Foxhound

The American foxhound is a serious working dog, bred and trained to track and hunt. But that doesn't mean she doesn't make for a fine house pet. She is gentle and friendly, although probably better suited to country life than being cooped up in an apartment or yard. Remember that she has been bred to keep up with galloping horses, so if you want to own her, be prepared to giddyup and go. She is also a scent hound. This means that once she has the line on a scent, almost nothing will draw her away from it. But foxhounds are super-smart, so if you are lucky enough to get one as a puppy, and work hard to train her, you can teach her to listen to you rather than her own stubborn instincts.

For more information on American foxhounds, check out: americanfoxhoundclub.org/FAQ.html

River view of Mount Vernon, circa 1801–1803, as painted by William Russell Birch